THE MOOD HOOVER

Written by Paul Brown

Illustrated by Rowena Blyth

fourth wall
publishing

Mischievous Stan was always
getting up to no good!

He also had a very special secret...

...he'd created an amazing machine
that could suck up anything
that was happy or fun.

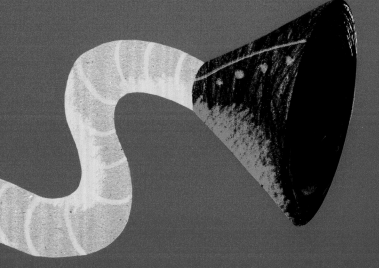

He'd proudly named his gizmo

'The Mood Hoover!'

And Stan was itching to try it out.

His sister's bedroom
was the perfect
place to test out
his invention.

Outside, a couple were admiring a huge, colorful rainbow up in the sky. Stan wasted no time and got straight to work.

Still sniggering to himself,
Stan made a quick escape.

At the Zoo, naughty Stan
sneaked his hoover past the man
in the ticket booth.

Inside there was so much color, happiness
and fun to choose from – Stan was spoilt for choice.

Then he spotted the perfect target!

"This will be simple!" thought Stan,
as he flicked the switch to 'ON'.

His machine immediately came to life and guzzled up
a little boy's ice cream... and all the Zebra's stripes!

Stan's hoover
sucked up
all the...

"This is so much fun,"
laughed Stan,
as he came across
another opportunity.

Down the street,
Stan could hear music
coming from the
Concert Hall.

Sneaking through the back door,
he placed his device
behind the large stage curtain...

On the bus,
Stan noticed a girl
wearing bright
red boots.

With her gum, she blew a

huge pink bubble!

...much to the horror
of the other passengers.

This made Stan
giggle out loud.

They both got off
at the stop by the park
and the girl bought some
colorful lollipops.

Stan was really itching
to cause more mayhem.

NEWS

THE TIMES   THE STANDARD

ZEBRA
LOSES
STRIPES

"Yuck! They look far too happy!"
said Stan, as he tried to start up his machine...
but nothing happened.

"It must be clogged up," he thought,
as he kicked it in frustration.

In the park, Stan noticed the girl admiring the flowers and suddenly they were surrounded by lots of beautiful, fluttering butterflies.

"Yuck! I hate butterflies!" said Stan.

Whirr, whirr, whirr!

Went the machine – but nothing happened!

"Why doesn't it work?"
muttered Stan
under his breath!

Determined to hoover
up the lollipop,
Stan set his machine
to maximum.

...but again,
nothing happened!

"Don't look so sad,
...this will
cheer you up."

said the girl
in the red boots.

Suddenly, there were lots
of flashing lights,
strange noises and smoke,
as the machine shook
out of control...

followed by
a gigantic explosion!

KA-BOOOM!!!

EMPTY

Instantly, Stan and the girl
were covered in a huge,
glittery shower of all
the beautiful things that the
hoover had gobbled up.

As they walked through the park the butterflies followed them...

...and Stan had forgotten all about his Mood Hoover!

The end